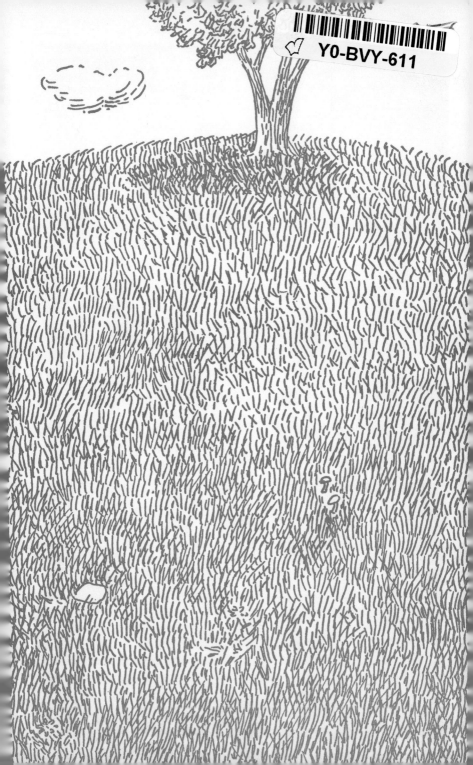

FELICIA

By the Same Author

Published by William Morrow and Company

BEACHCOMBER BOY

BELLS FOR A CHINESE DONKEY

THE BITTERN'S NEST

THE CHINESE DAUGHTER

CHRISTOPHER AND HIS TURTLE

COUSIN MELINDA

DAVY OF THE EVERGLADES

DEBORAH'S WHITE WINTER

DIANA IN THE CHINA SHOP

FAIR BAY

THE FIG TREE

THE FISHERMAN'S SON

HOLLY IN THE SNOW

INDIGO HILL

JANETTA'S MAGNET

JASPER

JEREMY'S ISLE

THE JOURNEY OF CHING LAI

LAURIE AND COMPANY

LITTLE PEAR AND THE RABBITS

THE LITTLE TUMBLER

LIVELY VICTORIA

MOLLY IN THE MIDDLE

THE MONKEY OF CROFTON

THREE LITTLE CHINESE GIRLS

WILLOW TREE VILLAGE

THE WONDERFUL GLASS HOUSE

WU, THE GATEKEEPER'S SON

THE YOUNGEST ARTIST

Published by Harcourt, Brace and Company

JUNIOR

LITTLE PEAR

LITTLE PEAR AND HIS FRIENDS

PEACHBLOSSOM

THE QUESTIONS OF LIFU

THE STORY OF LEE LING

FELICIA

ELEANOR FRANCES LATTIMORE

WILLIAM MORROW AND COMPANY

NEW YORK   1964

Contents

A Cat on the Doorstep

Charlotte was the only one in the Fairlee family who was fond of cats. She cut pictures of cats out of magazines and fastened them with thumbtacks to the wall above her bed. Persian kittens, tiger cats, and Siamese were all equally fascinating to Charlotte. But she had never been allowed to have a real, live cat, much as she wanted one.

There was no use in asking her parents why

she couldn't have a cat. Charlotte already knew what they would say. In the first place, her brother Tony was allergic to cats, as quite a few people are. When he was close to a cat he would start to sneeze, as if he had hay fever, or were coming down with a cold. That was one reason why cats were forbidden in the Fairlee household. Another reason was Bozo, the English sheep dog, who had a particularly strong feeling against cats.

Then there were the birds. The Fairlees lived in the country, and birds built nests in their orchard, year after year. Mrs. Fairlee loved birds, just as Charlotte loved cats, and she was afraid they would all fly away if a cat was accepted into her family. "Don't you like to hear the birds chirping?" she asked Charlotte.

"Yes, I do," said Charlotte. At the same time, she wished she could have a cat. There was one she often saw in a grocery store in Westover, when she went shopping with her mother. She never failed to look for it when she was in the store; she liked to pat it and hear it purr.

Late one summer a boy named John came to visit the Fairlees. His parents were friends of Dr. and Mrs. Fairlee, and he and Tony had been at camp together the month before. John's home was in another part of the state; but when his father and mother went to the mountains for their vacation, they dropped John off at the Fairlees' on their way, because the two boys wanted to see each other again.

"John says he can stay for two whole weeks," Tony announced. He was overjoyed, but Charlotte had a left-out feeling. She wished that John had a sister who was her age, so that she, also, could have a guest for two whole weeks.

That afternoon Charlotte said to her mother, "I wish I had a cat! Tony won't play with me now that John is here. But I wouldn't mind, if I had a cat to keep me company."

"You have Bozo," said her mother.

But Bozo was not a cat. He was a dog, and besides, he really belonged to Tony.

Bozo's favorite sleeping place was the kitchen, where he settled down after Mrs. Fairlee had washed the supper dishes. Dr. Fairlee had not come home for supper that night. He had telephoned to say that he had to make some house calls and would get himself a snack in Westover.

"I am going to wait for your father downstairs," said Mrs. Fairlee, when she came to tuck Charlotte into bed.

"Please, will you read me a bedtime story?" asked Charlotte. She knew how to read, but she wasn't too old to like having her mother read aloud to her.

"Very well. You can come downstairs in your pajamas, and I'll read to you in the living room," said her mother.

The boys were in Tony's room, where Tony was showing John his airplane models and other

prized possessions. Charlotte went downstairs, with a storybook under her arm, and seated herself beside her mother on the sofa. The evening was warm, so Mrs. Fairlee had left the windows open. She had left the front door open, too.

The story Charlotte wanted to hear that evening was about Dick Whittington and his cat. Her mother began to read it. She read several pages, and then she said, "Listen Charlotte, do you hear a car?"

Charlotte listened, but she didn't hear a single sound except for the soft, whispering stirrings of the summer night. She couldn't even hear Bozo snoring, as he often did, because the kitchen door was closed. "I don't hear anything. Please go on with the story," she said.

Mrs. Fairlee read another page or two. Then she paused again, and said, "I forgot to turn on the outside light."

Charlotte said, "I'll turn it on." She went to the front door, which opened into the living room, and switched on the light. To her surprise, she saw the shape of a cat through the screen wire. It was sitting up straight, and its two little ears had a listening look.

Charlotte tiptoed back to her mother. She didn't want to make any noise, for fear of scaring the cat away. "Mother," she whispered, "there is a nice cat on our doorstep."

Her mother smiled, and said, "How do you know it's nice?"

"It is sitting there so quietly," replied Charlotte. And she turned back toward the door.

"Please, dear, don't invite it into the house," said her mother.

No sooner had she spoken than the cat shape disappeared. Charlotte looked out, and saw nothing but the empty circle of light and the blackness of night beyond. "Oh, Mother, the cat has gone away," she said. "I think it heard what you said, and its feelings were hurt."

"It couldn't have understood me," said her mother.

"How do you know? It looked like a *clever* cat," said Charlotte. She wished she could have a clever, companionable cat, even though no one else in her family cared for cats.

Under the Elm Tree

The boys wanted to climb the hill behind the house the next morning, and Charlotte started off with them. The hill was steeper than it looked. Charlotte had climbed it any number of times, but its steepness always fooled her. She didn't want to admit that her legs were tired or that she was out of breath, but when she reached the shade of the lone elm tree she told

18

the boys that she was going to sit down for a while. "You don't have to wait for me, if you don't want to," she said.

Naturally, the boys didn't want to wait. Tony was in a hurry to show John the entire estate, which included the top of the hill. The Fairlee land ended on the far side of it, where a fence separated the grass-covered slope from a thickly grown wood.

The boys went on, leaving Charlotte under the tree. I wish I had a friend visiting *me*, she thought. It was hard for her to keep up with Tony and John. They were older than she was, and their legs were longer.

The elm tree was exactly halfway up the hill. Charlotte sat in its shade, with her arms around her knees, and looked down the slope toward her house. It looked like a toy house from where she sat, and the red barn looked like a toy too. She could see the roofs of Westover in the distance, and she could see the river curving like a snake. Far off were the mountains, where John's parents had gone. It was a beautiful view. But Charlotte was a little girl who didn't like to be all by herself. She said aloud, "I wish I had a friend visiting me!"

The tall grass near the elm tree parted, and a very dainty, middle-sized cat appeared. Charlotte had never seen a cat on the hillside before. Perhaps it's the same cat I saw last night, she thought.

The cat came nearer. Then it sat down and wrapped its tail around itself. It looked at Charlotte with grass-green eyes; its expression was reserved and at the same time expectant.

I mustn't hurt its feelings, whatever I do, thought Charlotte. This cat reminded her of the one she admired so much in the grocery store in Westover. Its small, triangular face was white, and the black markings on its head looked like black hair parted in the middle.

It's a calico cat, thought Charlotte. For that

was what her mother had called the grocery-store cat. There were spots of black and spots of yellow on its back, like printed calico cloth. "You are a very pretty cat—a calico cat," said Charlotte, who liked to talk to animals, even when she knew they couldn't reply. "Where do you live, kitty? If you belong in Westover, you've come a long way from home," Charlotte went on.

The cat turned its head and looked toward Westover. Charlotte noticed that the tip of its tail twitched slightly.

It seems to understand me, thought Charlotte. She got up from under the elm tree and moved softly toward the cat. It was obviously in no hurry to come close enough to be patted, but she knew that cats were different from dogs in that way. Bozo, for instance, was never happier than when someone was making a fuss over him. He was the same age as Tony; and although nine isn't very old for a boy, it is quite a great age for a dog. That was why Bozo didn't try to climb hills. He padded after the children through the house and around the garden, but he hardly ever went beyond the gate.

"I wish I could take you home with me, kitty," said Charlotte. "But there are a lot of birds around our place, and my mother loves birds."

The cat gave her a look with eyes so clear and honest that Charlotte felt sure *this* cat did not hunt birds. She said, apologetically, "Besides, my brother Tony sneezes whenever a cat is around. That's too bad, isn't it, kitty?"

"My name is not Kitty," said the cat.

Charlotte was so surprised that she touched the cat, quickly, to make sure that it was real and not something she had dreamed. Its fur was soft and silky, and perfectly real. "Say something more, if you know how to talk," said Charlotte.

"Well, to begin with, my name is Felicia,"

said the cat. "And I know what your name is. It's Charlotte Fairlee. Your brother's name is Tony, and the other boy's is John—the one who has just come to visit at your house."

Charlotte nodded. "How in the world did you know?" she asked. "Tell me, are you the same cat who was on our doorstep last night?"

"Yes. And it wasn't the first time, either," said Felicia. "I've often heard your mother reading you a bedtime story, when the windows were open. That foolish dog of yours is no kind of watchdog. I think it must sleep in the kitchen all night long."

"You mean Bozo. Yes, my mother lets him sleep in the kitchen, because he's so old," said Charlotte. "My mother thinks the world of Bozo."

Felicia said in a small, sad voice, "I haven't any mother. At least, I haven't seen her since I was a kitten. The people she lived with then wouldn't let her keep me. They gave me away to a little boy who pulled my tail, and I escaped as soon as I knew how to take care of myself."

"You poor little cat," said Charlotte. And the next thing she knew, Felicia had jumped into her lap. Charlotte stroked her between the ears. If only I could keep her, she thought.

"Perhaps you can come and visit me," she said. "I will explain to my mother that you won't harm the birds, and that you are a special sort of cat."

"*All* cats are special, Charlotte," said Felicia. "No, if your mother can't trust me, I had better stay away."

"Why?" said Charlotte. "If I told her that you can *talk*–"

"That's a secret, just between you and me," said Felicia. "Please don't mention it to anyone."

Charlotte promised not to, and Felicia began to purr. "You and I are friends, aren't we?" she said.

Just then Tony and John came running down the hill. Felicia sprang off Charlotte's lap and leaped away.

"Don't run away!" cried Charlotte. "Come back, Felicia!"

But by the time the two boys reached the elm tree, the calico cat had vanished.

Felicia Comes to Visit

Charlotte ran down the hillside after the boys. She was glad that neither of them had asked her any questions. She didn't want to break her promise to Felicia. Besides, Charlotte was wise enough to know that Tony and John would make fun of her if she told them that Felicia could talk. Talking cats have to be heard to be believed in.

I have a secret, I have a secret, Charlotte thought, as she went through the garden gate. The boys, once more, had left her behind, and she guessed that they had gone into the house.

The Fairlees' house was an old farmhouse that Dr. Fairlee had bought and remodeled. The sole inhabitant of its big red barn was a Shetland pony shared by Tony and Charlotte. The pony's name was Duke, and he was rarely in the barn during the summer months. He liked to roam around the fenced-in meadow, and when someone forgot to close the gate, he wandered into the shade of the orchard trees. Duke was not a bit interested in birds. They could fly in and out among the leaves without his bothering to turn his head.

Tony and Charlotte divided the responsibility of looking after Duke. Keeping the barn clean was their job, too, because their father had no time for work of that sort. Dr. Fairlee was a very busy man. He practiced in the village of

Westover and at the hospital in Linton, fifteen miles away. He was almost never at home except at night, and even then the telephone rang for him. Charlotte had once said to her mother, "Why is Father a doctor? If he were a farmer he could stay at home and farm our land, and Tony and I would help him."

"He wants to be a farmer when he retires," said Mrs. Fairlee. "That's why he bought this place."

Charlotte found her mother in the living room, arranging some flowers in a vase. "The boys have been in and out," she said to Charlotte. "There is a pitcher of lemonade in the kitchen, if you're thirsty."

"I'm very thirsty," said Charlotte. She went into the kitchen, proud of herself for not having told her secret. Bozo was lying on the kitchen linoleum with his head between his paws. "You aren't much of a watchdog, if you only knew," Charlotte said to him. Bozo gave a gentle snore, and opened one eye.

Three days passed; and although Charlotte kept looking, she saw no sign of her talking cat. Twice she went back to the elm tree and waited patiently, hoping that Felicia would appear. Once she went with her mother to Westover, where she asked Mr. Green, the grocer, about *his* cat. "She has a new set of kittens," Mr. Green informed her. "Don't you want to take home a couple of them, Charlotte?"

"Please don't offer her kittens, Mr. Green," said Mrs. Fairlee. "She would love them. But we can't have cats on account of our birds."

Charlotte looked for Felicia at night as well as in the daytime. While the boys were watching a television show, she opened the front door and peered out into the darkness. Then she went to the back door, and called softly, "Felicia!" But, if Felicia was nearby, she did not answer.

Charlotte had almost given up hope of seeing Felicia again, when one night, after her mother had read her a bedtime story, she heard a slight sound at the window—a sound like the scratching of a cat's claws. Her mother had gone out of the room and turned off the light. "Is that you, Felicia?" whispered Charlotte.

She jumped out of bed and went to the open window. At first she could see nothing beyond the screen wire. But when she pressed her face close to the screen, she saw two green eyes shining like two electric lights.

"Don't say a word. I am in a tree," whispered Felicia. "I came to say that I have a plan I want to tell you about, if you'll meet me on the hilltop tomorrow morning."

Charlotte put a finger to her lips. She nodded for yes, and then hopped back into bed.

It was Charlotte's turn to exercise Duke the next day, but she gladly gave her turn to John. She left the boys inside the barn, saddling the pony, and slipped out through the gate and started up the hill. She didn't have to tell her mother where she was going. She was as free

as a bird, because it was summer. Rules began when school began, and it wasn't schooltime yet.

The hill was as steep as ever, but Charlotte didn't stop to rest this time. She climbed and climbed, until she reached the very top; and there, sure enough, Felicia was waiting. She was crouched, catlike, on a moss-covered boulder. As soon as Charlotte came close to her, she stood up and stretched.

"I hope I didn't frighten you last night," said Felicia.

"No," said Charlotte. "I'd been looking for you."

"That was a good story your mother was reading. I prefer stories to television," said Felicia. Then she asked, "Do I look at all different from the way I did when you saw me before?"

"I don't think so," said Charlotte. "You're black and white and yellow, like Mr. Green's cat in Westover."

Felicia seemed disappointed, so Charlotte

added, "You're prettier than Mr. Green's cat, and you're smarter, because you talk like a girl."

"I want to *look* like a girl, too," declared Felicia. "That's the plan I want to tell you about. Do you think that if I looked like a little girl your mother would let me visit you?"

Charlotte tried not to laugh. She didn't see how a cat could possibly look like a little girl. But she didn't want to hurt Felicia's feelings, so she said, cautiously, "Yes, I think she might."

Felicia seemed to be satisfied with her answer. She smiled a cat smile, and then she said, "Well, if it's time for you to go home now, I will walk part way down the hill with you."

Charlotte liked being escorted by a cat. At first Felicia led the way, tail in air, but then she waited for Charlotte to catch up with her and rubbed against her legs. Charlotte patted her, and they walked on, side-by-side. All at once, Charlotte felt a soft little paw slip into her hand. She looked down. Felicia was walking on her hind legs!

"I've been practicing," said Felicia.

Charlotte was surprised. But she already knew that Felicia was a very unusual cat. They parted when they came to the elm tree, and Charlotte ran down the hill to her house.

That afternoon Mrs. Fairlee took the children to Westover to see a funny movie. There were animals in the movie, talking animals, and while Tony and John roared with laughter, Charlotte sat quietly, watching and listening. She wondered whether the boys would laugh or not if they knew about Felicia.

Her mother suggested a picnic a few days later. It was the day when her helper, Mrs. Crane, came to give the house its weekly cleaning, and she thought it would be a good idea to let her clean in peace. Mrs. Crane admitted that cleaning was easier without children underfoot. "I can fix my own lunch, if you'll take them away," she said to Mrs. Fairlee.

"Let's see," said Mrs. Fairlee. "Hard-boiled

eggs for Tony, and potato salad for Charlotte. John, what do you like to eat on picnics?"

John said that he liked sardine sandwiches.

Mrs. Fairlee looked in the kitchen cupboard to see if there was a tin of sardines. When she found one she said, "Everyone can be happy, because I'm going to pack a picnic lunch with something in it that each of you likes."

"You've forgotten yourself, Mother," said Charlotte. "What do you like on picnics?"

"Plenty of lemonade," said her mother.

Since the lunch basket was heavy and the pitcher of lemonade was hard to carry, Mrs. Fairlee and the children went no farther than the orchard. It was very pleasant there, with the birds chirping in the trees. Charlotte helped her mother spread a tablecloth on the grass, and Tony poured some lemonade into four paper cups.

They were about halfway through their lunch when Tony suddenly sneezed. "You're not

catching cold, are you, Tony?" said his mother. "Perhaps you had better run to the house and get your sweater."

It was just then that John said, speaking softly, "There is someone watching us."

Charlotte turned around quickly. There, partly hidden behind a tree, stood a little girl.

"Whose child is that, I wonder?" said Mrs. Fairlee. She called, "Come here, whoever you are. We have eaten up most of our picnic lunch, but we would be glad if you joined us."

The little girl came forward, shyly. "Thank you," she said. She was a very pretty little girl, about the same age as Charlotte. Her black hair was parted in the middle and tied at the sides with two perky bows. She wore a white cotton dress, dotted with yellow spots, and her little white feet were bare.

She reminds me of someone I know, thought Charlotte.

"What is your name, dear?" asked Mrs. Fairlee.

The little girl seemed to hesitate. Then she said, "Felicia," and she gave Charlotte a side-long look from her green eyes.

Charlotte clasped her hands together, and thought, My goodness me! She turned into a little girl!

The Green-Eyed Little Girl

Charlotte said, "Hello, Felicia." She tried to sound casual, even though her mind was in a whirl. She wondered if Felicia had really come to visit her, and if she was going to remain a little girl.

While she was wondering, her mother said, "You two girls seem to know each other."

Then she introduced Tony and John to Felicia, and offered Felicia a sandwich. "I hope you like sardines," she said.

"Indeed I do," said Felicia. "I can smell them a mile away! I was sure you must be having sardine sandwiches for your picnic, and I just had to come and see."

"We're very glad you came," said Mrs. Fairlee. But Tony and John were exchanging glances, and Tony murmured, "You and your sardines."

Charlotte thought that she ought to say something. She couldn't very well explain that Felicia was a cat, because she wasn't actually a cat any more. Felicia was her friend, although a queer little friend, and her green eyes were fixed on Charlotte with a hopeful expression. So Charlotte said, "Mother, I think it would be nice if Felicia visited us for a while."

"Yes, dear," said her mother, passing the potato salad. "I think it would be nice, too.

But we don't know whether Felicia's mother would let her come."

"I haven't any mother," said Felicia.

"Oh, I'm so sorry!" said Mrs. Fairlee. She set down the salad bowl and put her hand under Felicia's little pointed chin, looking down into her wistful face. "Where do you live then? I thought you must be one of the Hunter children, whose family rented the Gray cottage for the month of August."

Felicia said, "No, I'm all alone." She glanced at Charlotte, and added, "I haven't any home."

"But you must have a home," said Mrs. Fairlee. She turned to Charlotte, and asked, "Where did you see Felicia before?"

"On the hill," said Charlotte, truthfully.

"Yes, we met on the hillside," said Felicia.

The boys were getting restless. They had finished their lunch, and they weren't particularly interested in Charlotte's friend, or where Charlotte had met her. "Mother, will it be all

right if John and I go out to the meadow and
see Duke?" asked Tony.

He sneezed again. And his mother said, "Yes,
Tony, if you're sure you aren't catching cold."

The boys ran off, and Mrs. Fairlee and the
girls packed up the picnic things and shook out
the tablecloth. Mrs. Fairlee asked Felicia once
more about her home, thinking, of course, that
she must have one.

When Felicia again said that she had no
home, and no mother or father, Mrs. Fairlee invited her to stay for supper. "There's an extra
bed in Charlotte's room, and you can spend the
night, too," she said. "But I'm sure, Felicia,
that you belong to *somebody*. Dr. Fairlee will
be able to find your folks when he gets home."

Felicia took hold of Charlotte's hand and
held it tightly. She no longer had a soft paw,
but a little girl's fingers. "I can spend the night
and hear a bedtime story with you," she said.

Mrs. Fairlee answered for Charlotte. "We'll

see what Dr. Fairlee says. I don't want anyone to worry about you."

Felicia walked back to the house between Charlotte and her mother. Her step was light, and Charlotte thought, She has certainly practiced well! They left the picnic things on the kitchen table; and then Mrs. Crane called Mrs. Fairlee into the living room, to show her how nice the woodwork looked and how the chairs and tables gleamed with their new polish.

"Who is that little black-haired girl?" Mrs. Crane asked.

"I have no idea," said Mrs. Fairlee. "She says that she hasn't any home."

"She looks like a gypsy to me," said Mrs. Crane.

"Oh, no. She seems to be a nice little thing," said Mrs. Fairlee. "Children like to make up stories, and I don't believe for a minute that she is really homeless."

Charlotte, meanwhile, had taken Felicia up to

her room and showed her the bed where she was to sleep that night. "How did you manage it?" she asked Felicia.

"Partly because of watching you and practicing, and partly because of some special herbs I found in the woods," replied Felicia.

Charlotte looked puzzled. "Herbs?" she repeated.

"Yes," said Felicia. "You know those woods on the other side of the hill? Well, I've spent a lot of time there, and I experimented with tasting this little plant and that until I finally found a kind that made me look like a girl."

"I still don't understand," said Charlotte.

"You don't have to understand," said Felicia. "Come on, Charlotte. Let's not stay here and talk. Let's go out to the barn!"

"Duke isn't there," said Charlotte. "He's in the meadow."

"But there are mice in your barn. Have you ever chased mice?" said Felicia. "It's a lot of fun."

Charlotte said that she didn't intend to chase mice, ever. "If you are a girl, you must *act* like a girl," she said severely.

"All right," said Felicia. "What do you want to do?"

Charlotte said that she wanted to play with her dolls. She told Felicia that there was a lilac bush in the garden with the right amount of space beneath it for a doll's house. "It's a secret place of my own, but you can share it with me," she said.

"Will you keep *my* secret?" asked Felicia. "Will you promise not to tell your mother or anyone else who I am?"

Charlotte hesitated. She had planned to tell her mother. But if she told her mother, and Felicia was shooed away, that would be a mean thing to do. So she said, "I'll promise not to tell, if you promise not to chase mice or do other mischievous things that cats do sometimes."

"I'll *try* not to," said Felicia. Then she said,

briskly, "Now you can show me how to play with your dolls."

Mrs. Fairlee and Mrs. Crane were in the kitchen when the little girls went downstairs with their arms full of dolls. But Bozo was lying on the garden walk, and he gave a low growl when he saw Felicia.

"Don't pay any attention to Bozo. He often growls at strangers," said Charlotte.

"I have no use for dogs," said Felicia, stepping past Bozo. She followed Charlotte to the lilac bush, which made a fine playhouse. Charlotte told her the name of each of her dolls and showed her how to play with them. Felicia yawned after a while. She said that playing with dolls was almost the same as playing with kittens, except that you didn't have to bother to dress and undress kittens.

"That's the fun of playing with dolls—dressing them," said Charlotte. "No, Felicia! Don't pick them up by the backs of their necks!" She laughed, and Felicia laughed. Anyone hearing them would have thought that they were both everyday, ordinary, little girls.

Dr. Fairlee did not return home that night until after Mrs. Fairlee had given the children their supper. He had had a busy day at the hospital in Linton. When Mrs. Fairlee asked him what should be done about Felicia, the strange little girl who had suddenly appeared, all he said was, "I'll try to locate her people in the morning. She's a pretty little thing."

"Yes, she is," said Mrs. Fairlee. "Did you notice her eyes?"

"They were the first thing I noticed about her," said Dr. Fairlee. "Just as green as a cat's."

Bozo Becomes a Watchdog

The television set was turned on in the living room, and Tony and John were watching a Western program that had a lot of shooting in it. Whenever someone on the screen fired a gun, Tony and John cried, "Bang, bang!" They were both armed with pistols, but they didn't fire them, because they were water pistols. They had wanted to have a water fight outdoors, but Mrs. Fairlee had put a stop to that idea. "It's too late for outdoor play," she said.

Charlotte and Felicia lingered downstairs until Mrs. Fairlee said, "It's your bedtime, Charlotte, and I think it must be Felicia's bedtime, too. You will have to lend her a pair of your pajamas."

"Yes, Mother. I'll lend her my pink ones," said Charlotte.

The girls went upstairs, and Charlotte took her pink pajamas out of her bureau drawer and handed them to Felicia. "You can have the first bath, if you like," she said.

Felicia gave a little shudder, and said, "I don't like water unless I'm thirsty."

"But you have to take baths to keep clean," protested Charlotte.

"I'm perfectly clean," replied Felicia.

Charlotte looked her over carefully. There was no denying that Felicia was spotless.

"Well, my mother insists that I have a bath every single night," she said.

"Why? You don't look dirty to me," said Felicia.

"Of course, I'm not really dirty," said Charlotte. She went into the bathroom and turned on the water taps. Then she thought that, after all, it wasn't necessary for her to have a bath that night. She had washed her hands just before supper, and, as Felicia said, she didn't look dirty. . . . I'll skip my bath, she thought. So she turned off the water and got into her pajamas. She and Felicia were both in their beds when Mrs. Fairlee came upstairs to check on them.

"My! How quick you were," said Mrs. Fairlee. She asked, suspiciously, "Are you sure you both bathed?"

There was a guilty silence. Then Charlotte said, "We didn't think we needed to have baths tonight, Mother, because we were perfectly clean."

Mrs. Fairlee looked annoyed. She felt quite sure that skipping baths must have been Felicia's idea. But she didn't want to scold Felicia. Felicia was not her child. She said, looking at Charlotte, "I'm not sure that you girls deserve a story tonight."

"Oh, please read to us, Mother," begged Charlotte. "Felicia has been looking forward to a story."

Mrs. Fairlee picked up the book that Charlotte had hopefully placed on the table beside her bed. She sat down, and began to read the story, *Puss in Boots*. While she was reading, the doctor put his head in at the door. He said that he had just received a call from one of his patients, and that he had to go back to Linton that night. "I will take Bozo along with me in the car," he said. "Poor fellow, he seems very restless for some reason."

"Yes, I've noticed that," said Mrs. Fairlee.

The doctor said he would get home as early

as possible, and went down the stairs. Mrs. Fairlee finished reading the girls their story. Charlotte knew *Puss in Boots* backward and forward, but it was new to Felicia, and she listened wide-eyed. "Thank you," she said, as Mrs. Fairlee turned off the light. "That was a lovely story, Mrs. Fairlee!"

"Sleep tight, both of you," said Mrs. Fairlee.

Charlotte had almost gone to sleep when she heard a cat yowling outdoors. The yowling came from rather far away at first, but as she listened, it grew louder and louder, as if the cat was approaching the house.

"I can't go to sleep with that awful noise," she said.

"What awful noise?" asked Felicia, who was wide awake.

"That yowling," said Charlotte.

"Why, it's just a cat, announcing his presence," said Felicia.

"What do you mean, *announcing his pres-*

ence?" said Charlotte. "I call that yowling."

The yowling was very loud indeed now. Charlotte put her fingers in her ears, but Felicia jumped out of her bed and went to the window.

It was a beautiful, starry night. Charlotte watched Felicia, who seemed to be trying to push up the window screen. She took her fingers out of her ears, and asked, "What are you doing, Felicia?"

Felicia sighed. "I guess I can't get out this way," she said. "But oh, Charlotte, I do want to go outdoors! All cats like the dark. Don't you like it, too?"

"I haven't been out in the dark very often," said Charlotte.

The cat outside yowled again. Felicia went over to Charlotte's bed, and said, "Let's go out in the dark together. We can slip down the stairs, and I don't think anyone will hear us, because the boys are still watching television and they have it turned on loud."

"We can't go out," said Charlotte.

"Why not?" said Felicia. "Your father took Bozo in the car with him, and we can go out by the kitchen door."

They *could* do that, thought Charlotte. And what fun it would be! Almost before she knew it, she was out of bed and tiptoeing down the stairs with Felicia. No one heard them go out through the kitchen door.

In the living room, the boys had just turned off the television, and they, too, were able to hear the yowling cat. In spite of the fact that Mrs. Fairlee had told them to go to bed, they looked at each other and gripped their water pistols.

"A cat," said Tony.

"Let's get him," said John.

They dashed outside, and, at that precise moment, Charlotte and Felicia came around to the front of the house. Charlotte didn't see the

cat. She saw Tony and John, who couldn't wait to use their water pistols. "Duck!" she cried to Felicia.

She and Felicia ducked, but not before they were hit by two sprays of water. Felicia gave an anguished cry, and Charlotte said crossly, "What do you boys mean by shooting us with those pistols?"

"What are you two girls doing out here?" demanded Tony.

"Charlotte! Felicia!" said Mrs. Fairlee, who had stepped outdoors to see what all the fuss was about. She was really annoyed this time. She sent the girls back upstairs, and told the boys to put away their water pistols and to get ready for bed.

"The cat has gone away," she said, which must have been true, because it didn't yowl any more.

It was after midnight when Dr. Fairlee returned home. The house was dark except for the light above the front door, and everyone was asleep. He said at the breakfast table the next morning, "I didn't hear a sound last night. But Bozo jumped out of the car as soon as I opened the door, and began sniffing all around the house."

"There was a cat prowling around here," said Mrs. Fairlee.

"He was *yowling* around, wasn't he, John?" said Tony.

"It's a long time since we've been troubled by cats," said Dr. Fairlee. "Perhaps we had better start putting Bozo outdoors again at night. He used to be a good watchdog, and it seems as if he still wants to be one."

Tony sneezed.

"What makes you sneeze?" asked his father. "Are you sure that cat isn't still around?"

Charlotte squeezed Felicia's hand under the table, and watched her father's face anxiously. She felt relieved when he said, "Perhaps you have hay fever, Tony. I noticed yesterday that they have started to mow the fields between here and Westover."

Dr. Fairlee went off to the hospital, and Mrs. Fairlee began to clear away the breakfast dishes. She tried to make Bozo go outdoors, but Bozo wouldn't go. He kept looking at Felicia, and growling.

Bozo knows that Felicia is really a cat, thought Charlotte. She was afraid that Bozo might become *too* good a watchdog.

Duke Jumps over the Fence

Charlotte and Felicia helped Mrs. Fairlee with the dishes. Mrs. Fairlee washed them, Charlotte dried them, and Felicia took each plate and cup that Charlotte dried and set it carefully on the kichen table. All of Felicia's motions were quick and graceful, and her bare feet made no sound on the linoleum-covered floor. Charlotte had offered to lend her a pair of her shoes, but Felicia said that she preferred to go barefoot. "It seems more natural," she said.

Charlotte was pleased that Felicia was helping in the kitchen. She had tied an apron around her waist, and her black hair lay smooth and glossy on her shoulders. "She is just like a little girl," Charlotte said to herself. But at that moment Felicia suddenly crouched down on the floor, and gazed intently at a spot between the sink and the stove. "S-sh—I think I hear a mouse," she whispered.

Mrs. Fairlee spoke rather sharply. "There aren't any mice in my kitchen, Felicia. Please get up off the floor."

Charlotte could tell that her mother was both displeased and puzzled by Felicia's behavior. I hope that Mother won't guess, she thought, as Felicia stood up. She shook her head at Felicia when her mother's back was turned, and said loudly, "Of course, there aren't any mice here."

The boys had been out in the barn, saddling Duke. Charlotte, from the window, saw them leading him into the backyard, and she heard John say, "It's your turn for the first ride, Tony."

But it wasn't Tony's turn. It was Charlotte's, and Charlotte decided that she would give her turn to Felicia. "How would you like to ride our pony?" she asked her. "Come, we'd better hurry, or Tony will ride him first."

"I've never ridden a pony before," said Felicia.

"Run along," said Mrs. Fairlee, who knew that Duke was a very gentle pony, besides being midget-sized.

The girls ran out of the house, and Bozo pushed past them and padded up to Duke, whom he sniffed politely. They were good friends, although they didn't have much in common.

"It's my turn, and I'm giving my turn to Felicia," announced Charlotte.

Duke danced sideways. He was frisky that morning, and his eyes gleamed from under his long bangs.

Tony said to John, "Charlotte is right. It's her turn, and she can give it to anyone she chooses." Then he asked Felicia, "Do you know how to ride?"

Felicia shook her head.

"Well, all you have to do is sit tight in the saddle, and sort of grip with your knees," said Tony. He helped Felicia up into the saddle, and showed her what to do with the reins and bridle. "You mustn't pull on the bridle, because that will hurt Duke's mouth. Just slap him on the back if you want him to go fast," he said.

"*I* want to tell Felicia what to do," said Charlotte. "Stop barking, Bozo!" For Bozo was barking at Felicia. "Let me hold the bridle for you, Felicia," Charlotte continued. She wanted to lead Duke around the backyard, at a walk, until Felicia became used to riding him.

But Charlotte didn't have time to catch hold

of the bridle, because Bozo snapped at Duke's heels, and the pony dashed away. "Bozo!" shouted Tony. He grabbed Bozo by the collar. But neither he nor John nor Charlotte could do a thing about Duke. Just as Bozo had never behaved so rudely before, Duke had never tried to run away. But it looked now, as if that was exactly what he was doing. He galloped off, with Felicia clinging to his back, and disappeared around the corner of the house.

Charlotte ran in pursuit, vainly crying, "Stop!"

Tony, with John's help, dragged Bozo into the house, and then they hurried after Charlotte to see what was happening. Duke had charged through the open gate into the meadow, and Felicia, with her hair flying, sat lightly in the saddle.

"He hasn't thrown her yet," said John.

"He'd better not!" cried Charlotte.

"Watch—he's heading straight toward that

back fence!" cried Tony. The wire fence was invisible from a distance, but Tony knew it was there, and he knew that it was high.

Charlotte knew, too, and she said, breathlessly, "He'll have to stop running when he gets to the fence."

"Yes, he'll certainly have to turn back," said John.

However, Duke did not turn back. He jumped over the fence! And, as he did so, Felicia sailed off his back—and landed, miraculously, on her feet.

"Did you see that?" cried John.

Charlotte didn't reply, because she had started running toward Felicia. Tony didn't reply, either. He was running to capture Duke, who, after he had got rid of his rider, was peacefully munching grass on the far side of the fence.

"Were you hurt, Felicia?" asked Charlotte, when she was near enough to speak to her.

"Not a bit, because I landed on my feet,"

said Felicia. She was smiling her cat smile, and she added, proudly, "I always land on my feet."

Tony squeezed under the fence and caught hold of Duke's bridle. Charlotte saw him climb into the saddle, and she wondered if he expected Duke to jump the fence again. But Duke was now as gentle as a lamb—or as gentle as he had always been until that morning. He refused to jump the fence, which made things awkward for Tony. He had to ride him home by a roundabout route, and dismount in order to go through a little-used gate that was closed with a piece of barbed wire.

Tony was cross with both Felicia and Charlotte. He said that Felicia shouldn't have ridden Duke if she didn't know how to handle a pony, and that Charlotte shouldn't have let her. "If she *had* to ride, why didn't you let me teach her?" he said to Charlotte. "Duke never acted that way before, and it's all because you girls got him rattled."

"No, it was because of Bozo," Charlotte said. She was quite sure that Duke wouldn't have run away and jumped the fence and thrown Felicia off his back, if Bozo hadn't begun snapping at his heels the minute Felicia was in the saddle.

The Flight of the Birds

Mrs. Fairlee had been planning to have a party for John on the last day of his visit, but she hadn't told the children about it yet. While they were all out of earshot she called up two friends of hers, and invited their boys, George and Philip, to come to the party. They accepted for the boys; and then Mrs. Fairlee called up another friend, who was the mother of twin girls. "Can Mary and Susy come to a children's party on Friday afternoon?" she asked.

"I am sure they would love to come," said the twins' mother.

"That's fine," said Mrs. Fairlee. "By the way, do you happen to know of a little girl named Felicia? She appeared yesterday, apparently from nowhere, while the children and I were having a picnic, and she insists that she hasn't any family."

"What is her last name?" asked the twins' mother.

"If she knows, she hasn't told us," said Mrs. Fairlee. "She's an odd little girl, in many ways."

"Odd?" repeated her friend.

"Yes. It's hard to explain, but she doesn't behave quite like other children," said Mrs. Fairlee.

The twins' mother said that Felicia sounded

interesting and asked if she was going to be at the party.

"Oh, yes, unless her family comes to fetch her," said Mrs. Fairlee. "My husband is going to make inquiries today to see if he can find out anything about her. He knows all the authorities because of his work at the hospital."

When Mrs. Fairlee had finished telephoning, she looked out her upstairs window and listened to the birds, twittering and chirping in the trees. She had been too busy in the house to see Duke's mad dash, and all the excitement in the meadow had been too far away for her to hear. All she saw was Charlotte and Felicia strolling off together toward the orchard. Their heads were close together, as if they were whispering secrets.

Charlotte was saying to Felicia, "Tony is cross, and John always sides with him, so let's not pay any attention to them. I haven't showed you our swing yet. It's in the orchard, near where we had our picnic."

"Is swinging more exciting than riding?" asked Felicia.

"That all depends," said Charlotte. "I can swing upside down, and I can skin the cat, too."

Felicia shuddered, and Charlotte said, "I don't really mean that. What I mean is turning a sort of somersault on the swing."

The orchard was the birds' special nesting place. Charlotte had forgotten about that in her eagerness to show Felicia the swing. Actually, the nest-building time was long past, and the baby birds that had grown up in the orchard were fat robins now, or long-tailed jays, or bright-colored woodpeckers. They kept busy with their own lives, looking for worms and pecking away for insects, and no one ever bothered them.

"Look at me!" cried Charlotte, hanging upside down in the swing. "Can you do this, Felicia?"

But Felicia was not watching her.

Charlotte called again, "Look, Felicia!"

Felicia stood motionless. She was watching a robin. It was down on the ground, hop-hopping toward her, completely occupied with its business of looking for a worm.

Charlotte didn't see her mother coming down the path, and neither did Felicia. There was a flutter of wings as Felicia suddenly pounced. "I've got him, Charlotte!" she cried triumphantly.

"Felicia!" scolded Charlotte. "Let go of that bird this minute! Didn't I tell you not to do mischievous things?"

"Felicia!" Mrs. Fairlee swooped down upon her, and Felicia was so surprised that she let go of the bird.

"I'm sorry," she said meekly. But her eyes followed the robin as it flew away to safety on a high tree limb.

"Don't you ever do such a thing again, Felicia," said Mrs. Fairlee. She was more than annoyed this time. She was deeply shocked.

Felicia slipped away to the swing. Her expression was thoughtful, but she didn't look as sorry as she ought to have looked. She swung slowly at first, and then she swung very high, so high that her toes nearly touched the leaves of the tree above her. Charlotte, watching her, felt very puzzled indeed. How can a girl keep acting like a cat, or a cat be so much like a girl? she wondered. After her mother had gone back to the house, she said, "I think I ought to tell my mother about you, Felicia. It wasn't fair of you to pounce on that poor robin."

"Why not?" said Felicia. "Your mother pounced on *me*. Wasn't that exactly the same thing?"

"It wasn't a bit the same," said Charlotte. But she felt troubled and more mixed-up than before.

When Dr. Fairlee came home that evening he told Mrs. Fairlee that he had been unable to find out anything about Felicia or her family.

No one had reported losing a little girl. No one had seen or heard of a little girl who fitted his description of Felicia. "We will have to keep her with us for the time being," he said.

"I suppose we'll have to," said Mrs. Fairlee. She looked very unhappy, and the doctor said, "What's the matter? Felicia isn't any trouble, is she? From what I've seen of her so far, she is well-mannered. And Charlotte seems to like her."

Mrs. Fairlee said that Charlotte liked her, but that Felicia was by no means an ideal play-mate for her. She told him that Felicia had caught a bird that morning, which seemed to her decidedly cruel. "Of course, she may not have known any better," she added. "Poor Felicia! Do you suppose that she really has no family? I thought at first that she was making that up."

"She may be a victim of amnesia," said the doctor.

After supper that night Mrs. Fairlee told Charlotte and Felicia that she wasn't going to read them a bedtime story. She also said there was to be no nonsense about baths, and she went upstairs with them to supervise their baths herself.

"We aren't babies, Mother," protested Charlotte.

"No, you are naughty girls," said her mother. Then she turned her attention to Felicia, and gave her a very thorough scrubbing. Felicia submitted to the scrubbing, but she shivered so much and looked so miserable that Mrs. Fairlee relented, and said she would read a story, after all.

The story she read was about Aladdin and his wonderful lamp. It took Charlotte's mind away from troubling thoughts, and it made Felicia cheerful again. Felicia thanked Mrs. Fairlee when she had finished reading, and then she curled up in her bed and went to sleep like a kitten.

It was a quiet night. There was no barking, no yowling. But, in the morning, there were no chirping sounds either. All of the birds had departed from the orchard, leaving nothing but their old, empty nests behind them.

"Our lovely birds have all flown away!" cried Mrs. Fairlee. She looked at Felicia accusingly, and Felicia lowered her eyes. Charlotte felt torn between her mother and her friend. She knew that the birds had flown away on account of Felicia, but she couldn't bring herself to excuse Felicia by explaining to her mother that she was a cat. That was Felicia's secret, and Felicia was her friend.

The Shopping Trip

It was Thursday, and the party was to be the next afternoon. When Mrs. Fairlee told the children they were going to have a party, they were all very excited. "We'll play games, won't we, Mother? And have prizes?" said Tony.

"Please, Mother, will you make a cake?" asked Charlotte.

Mrs. Fairlee said that of course she would

bake a cake, and Felicia said softly, "A party. A children's party."

Mrs. Fairlee didn't have time to grieve about the birds that morning. She had to plan for the party. The cake could be baked the next day, but in the meantime she must drive to Westover to buy the party favors and the prizes for the games. She sat down at her desk to write a shopping list, and Charlotte appeared at her elbow. "Mother, may I wear my Sunday dress at the party, and my ruffled petticoat?" asked Charlotte.

"Yes, Charlotte," said her mother.

"And I want to wear bows on my hair, like Felicia's," added Charlotte. She admired Felicia's hair ribbons, which stood up perkily on each side of her head. Rather like ears, thought Charlotte.

Felicia came and stood beside Mrs. Fairlee's other elbow, and asked, "What shall I wear to the party?" She had only one dress of her own the white dress with yellow polka dots on it. Charlotte had offered to lend her a pink dress, or a blue one, but until now Felicia had said that she liked her own dress better.

A party, though, was another matter. Mrs. Fairlee said that Felicia needed a party dress, and she told the girls that she would take them with her to Westover, where Felicia could pick out a dress for herself. "What color do you think you would like?" she asked Felicia.

"I would like a striped dress," said Felicia.

"Red and white stripes?" asked Charlotte.

"No. Brown and yellow stripes. Or else plain black," said Felicia.

Cat colors, thought Charlotte.

Her mother said, "Goodness me, Felicia! You don't want to wear *black*. You aren't in mourning for anyone."

"Is mourning the same as yowling?" asked Felicia.

"Felicia!" cried Charlotte.

"I was just joking," said Felicia. She rubbed her head against Mrs. Fairlee's arm.

"Don't be silly, Felicia," said Mrs. Fairlee, impatiently. Her expression, as she drew her arm away from Felicia, made Charlotte wonder if she had guessed Felicia's secret. She took hold of Felicia's hand in a protective way, and, for the first time, noticed how sharp her nails were.

The boys wanted to go to Westover, too. They didn't have any real shopping to do, but they each had a little pocket money, and they thought they might like to buy some comic books and maybe some ice-cream cones. With the girls, they piled into Mrs. Fairlee's old station wagon. The girls sat up in front with Mrs. Fairlee, and the boys sat in the back. They left Bozo on guard in front of the house.

Tony sneezed and sneezed. But it was the haying season, so no one made any remarks about it. Charlotte started to count the haystacks in the fields they passed; but she forgot the haystacks when her mother said that since Felicia might be their guest for a week or more, she had better buy her some school clothes as well as a party dress. "And you must have some shoes, Felicia," said Mrs. Fairlee. "It's going to be time for school before you know it."

"School?" said Felicia. She sounded so surprised that Charlotte turned to look at her. Felicia was quite pale, and she sat very tensely—almost as if she were ready to spring out of the car.

Of course, Felicia has never been to school, thought Charlotte. But I will introduce her to my teacher, and I will help her if she has a hard time. "You will like the Westover school, Felicia," she said hopefully.

There was no reply from Felicia.

"Here we are," said Mrs. Fairlee. For they had reached the village of Westover. There was only one shopping street in the village. The clothing stores and the grocery stores were huddled close together and behind them was a parking lot. Mrs. Fairlee parked the car, and told the children to hop out. The girls were to stay with her, but she said that the boys could roam around wherever they pleased while she bought clothes for Felicia and did her other errands. "Be sure to come back to the car in an hour," she said. "It is ten o'clock now."

"All right, Mother," said Tony. He and John strolled off, fingering their pocket money.

Although Felicia was often a trial to Mrs. Fairlee, she was on her best behavior in the dress shop, where Mrs. Fairlee took her to be outfitted. She picked out a full-skirted yellow dress to wear to the party, and then she let Mrs. Fairlee select two school dresses for her.

Shopping for shoes, however, was a great deal harder. Felicia at first refused to try on any shoes, declaring that she had never worn shoes in her life. Mrs. Fairlee was embarrassed, and

the clerk was discouraged, as pair after pair of shoes was put back on the shelf.

"How about sneakers?" asked Charlotte.

That was an inspiration, because Felicia finally settled on a pair of white sneakers. She put them on and walked back and forth in front of a mirror. The sneakers were as noiseless as bare feet, as noiseless as cats' feet.

"They aren't at all suitable for a party, but I suppose they will have to do," said Mrs. Fairlee.

After they left the shoe store, Mrs. Fairlee took the girls into another shop, where she bought everything that was needed for the party. She let Charlotte and Felicia pick out the favors, and she herself chose the prizes while their backs were turned. Then Mrs. Fairlee said, "Since we are here, let's go into the grocery store for a minute. I noticed that Mr. Green has a sign in his window saying that he has fresh fish today."

"Yum-yum," said Felicia.

"Oh, Felicia, maybe we'll have a chance to see Mr. Green's cat," said Charlotte.

The cat was not in the window, where it often sat. It was at the rear of the store, peacefully lying on a crate of oranges. Charlotte spied it almost immediately, and she said, "There it is! Come, Felicia." She left her mother talking to Mr. Green and walked toward the cat. Felicia followed her, after pausing for a moment in front of the fish counter.

"Nice kitty," said Charlotte, patting the calico cat. "How are your new kittens? Has Mr. Green found homes for them all?"

To her surprise, the cat suddenly sat alert. Felicia had walked up quietly in her sneakers, and the cat was staring at her, not at Charlotte. Then it made some little murmuring, burping sounds. Charlotte could not be certain, but she was almost sure that it was talking to Felicia.

Felicia leaned close to the calico cat, so close that its whiskers brushed her face. She was making whispering sounds that Charlotte couldn't understand.

"What are you saying?" she asked Felicia.

But neither Felicia nor the calico cat seemed to realize that Charlotte was there. Green eyes looked into green eyes. Whispers purred back and forth. "Come, Felicia," said Charlotte impatiently, taking hold of her hand.

"Come, Charlotte and Felicia!" called her mother. "It's past eleven, so we'd better go and meet the boys."

Felicia finally turned away from the cat on the orange crate, and went out to the parking lot with Charlotte and her mother.

The Party

Charlotte didn't have a moment alone with Felicia until they were back at the house again. Felicia eyed Bozo, who was lying on the front steps, and said, "Let's go in by the back door."

"Here, Felicia, carry your dresses upstairs," said Mrs. Fairlee, handing her the package from the dress shop.

As soon as they were in their room, Charlotte asked, "Were you and that cat talking to each other?"

"Yes. She happens to be my mother," said Felicia.

Charlotte sat down, hard, on the edge of her bed. She had noticed, of course—when Felicia still looked like a cat—that she resembled the cat in Mr. Green's store. But it had never occurred to her that they were related. "Your *mother*," she repeated. "You told me, Felicia, that you hadn't seen your mother since you were a kitten."

"That's perfectly true," replied Felicia. "Today was the first time I had seen her since I was given away to that horrid little boy. But she recognized me immediately."

"How queer!" said Charlotte.

"I don't see anything queer about that," said Felicia. Then, changing the subject, she said, "I want to look at my party dress." She opened the package and lifted it out, smoothing its skirt with loving little pats.

"I think your school dresses are pretty, too," said Charlotte.

"You may have them, if you like," said Felicia. "I have no intention of going to school and being bossed around by a teacher. Whoever heard of a cat going to school?"

"But no one, except me, knows that you're a cat," said Charlotte. "I haven't told a single person, not even my mother."

"I know," said Felicia. "You're a real friend, Charlotte. But I won't go to school, even to please you."

Charlotte began to feel doleful at the prospect of school again. Her teacher *was* very bossy, she thought.

Mrs. Fairlee was almost in despair by the time Dr. Fairlee came home that evening. She told him that her newest trouble was Felicia's

refusal to go to school. "What's more, Charlotte says that she doesn't like school and wants
to stay at home this year," she said.

"That's nonsense," said the doctor, firmly.
"Both girls will have to go to school. In the
meantime, I'm going to continue my efforts to
find Felicia's family."

A special, festive air hung over the house the
next day. The party feeling began when the
cake was in the oven and when Mrs. Fairlee set
the table, putting a fancy paper hat beside each
place. "Four boys and four girls," she said
aloud.

"Mary and Susy are the girls you invited,
aren't they?" said Charlotte.

"Yes. And the boys are George and Philip,"
said her mother. She put a party favor beside
each paper hat. Then she went into the kitchen
to take the cake out of the oven. Charlotte and
Felicia watched while she made the frosting.

The boys, meanwhile, were coaxing Bozo into the cellar, so that he wouldn't bother any of the guests.

The first guests to arrive were George and Philip. Their mothers brought them, but the mothers didn't stay. They said that they had to go to a club meeting, but that they would come back for the boys at six o'clock.

The mother of the twin girls, who arrived soon afterward, stayed to keep Mrs. Fairlee company. The little girls, Mary and Susy, rushed up to Charlotte, and she introduced them to Felicia.

"Oh, is this Felicia?" asked their mother. She shook hands with Felicia, who looked demure and pretty in her yellow party dress.

The two mothers seated the children at the dining table, cut the cake, and brought sandwiches in from the kitchen. They waited to see that each child had put on a paper hat, and then they went into the living room to have their

own cake and sandwiches. The prizes for the children's games were on a little table, and tacked against the wall was a cardboard donkey, waiting to have paper tails pinned to it.

"I don't see anything wrong with Felicia," said the twins' mother. "She curtseyed when she shook hands with me, just like Charlotte."

"She's a little copycat," said Mrs. Fairlee. She added that Felicia's manners were usually nice, but that she had some very peculiar notions.

"She's a pretty child," said the twins' mother.

"Yes. I only hope that she won't upset the party in some way," said Mrs. Fairlee.

The children, in the dining room, were discussing games. Tony told the guests that he and John had laid out a treasure hunt that morning. The clues were upstairs, downstairs, and in the kitchen.

"I like treasure hunts, and I like follow-the-leader," said George.

"What do you like to play?" Mary asked Felicia.

"Cat's cradle and pussy wants a corner," said Felicia.

"Those are baby games," said Susy.

They are cat games, thought Charlotte. She said, "I'm sure that Felicia knows how to play hide-and-seek." Which happened to be her own favorite game.

"It's all right, but I like sardines better," said Philip.

Felicia said that she liked sardines better, too, and Charlotte nudged her gently. She was sure that Felicia was thinking of the sardines you eat instead of the game sardines.

When the children had finished eating they trooped into the living room. Mrs. Fairlee blindfolded them each in turn, spun them around, and told them to pin a tail on the donkey. John was the winner of that game, and he received a prize.

"Let's have the treasure hunt next," suggested Tony.

"The treasure hunt! The treasure hunt!" cried Susy and Mary, as he handed out the slips of paper on which he had written the clues. Easy as the clues were, Felicia could not read hers, and she stood holding her slip of paper while all the other children dashed upstairs.

"What's the matter, Felicia?" asked the twins' mother. She looked at the writing on the paper she held, and said, "You'd better hurry. The next clue is upstairs in Tony's wastebasket."

Felicia hurried off, and Mrs. Fairlee shook her head over her apparent backwardness. She had no idea what the real trouble was until her friend said, in a very puzzled voice, "I don't believe that Felicia knows how to read."

"I never thought of that," said Mrs. Fairlee. "She has set her mind against going to school, and perhaps that's why. Do you see what I mean about Felicia's being strange? A child of her age surely ought to know how to read."

The twins' mother agreed with her, and said
that she wondered what Felicia's family back-
ground was like.

George won the treasure hunt. After he had
been given his prize, he asked if they could play
follow-the-leader next. "I really ought to take
Mary and Susy home," said the twins' mother.
"It's getting late, and I have supper to prepare."

"Just one more game, Mother," pleaded the
twins. But follow-the-leader, which was played
outdoors, was not the last game. The twins'
mother took them home after it was over, but
the mothers of George and Philip had not come
for them yet. That was why, finally, the children who remained started to play sardines.
The afternoon was darkening, but the boys all
said sardines was best when it was played in the
dark.

Charlotte saw that Felicia looked bewildered,
so she explained the rules to her. "Sardines is

just the opposite from hide-and-seek, because the person who is It is the one who hides," she said. "If you are It, Felicia, you must stay in your hiding place, and when we find you we pile in after you—like a row of sardines."

"The last person to find the hiding place is It next time," said John. "Do you understand?"

Felicia nodded. "I understand perfectly," she said. "Can you hide anywhere you choose?"

"Anywhere in the garden or in the house," said Tony. "It wouldn't be fair, of course, to hide way out in the meadow."

Tony counted out to see who was It, and the one who was It turned out to be Felicia. "All right," said Tony, "Shut your eyes, everybody, while I count to a hundred." He counted out loud, and Charlotte, with her eyes tight shut, tried to imagine what hiding place Felicia would choose. Cats are good hiders, and they like the dark, she thought. . . . When she opened her eyes, Felicia had vanished soundlessly.

Two of the boys, John and Philip, looked for her in the house. Tony, George, and Charlotte looked for her in the garden, where every shadow could serve as a hiding place at that time of the evening. They searched separately and stealthily, because each of them wanted to find Felicia first and hide with her from the others.

It was rather scary in a way, Charlotte thought. The familiar garden was becoming very dark. She looked under the lilac bush. Felicia was not there. Then she ventured into the orchard and looked behind each tree. The trees loomed like dark giants in the dusk, the grass was wet with dew, and there was no sign of Felicia.

Where *is* she? Charlotte wondered. She ran back toward the house, and saw that someone, probably her mother, had turned on the lights. She caught a glimpse of Tony darting through the front door. Perhaps Felicia is in the house, and Tony will find her, she thought.

Then a new idea came to her. She had forgotten the barn, because Tony hadn't mentioned it when he was naming the places where it would be fair to hide. But Charlotte remembered that Felicia liked the barn, and she knew that it was full of hiding places. Duke occupied only one of the stalls, and there was the hayloft and an old farm wagon.

Charlotte went into the barn just as a car drove up to the house. She didn't stop to think that George and Philip's mothers had come for them and that the party was over. She left the door open behind her, and in the dim light she saw Felicia, who was in the barn all by herself. Felicia was not aware of her. She held something in her hands, and Charlotte guessed at once that she had captured a mouse.

"Drop it!" she cried.

But Felicia kept her prize until Charlotte caught hold of her wrists and forced her fingers apart. The mouse skittered away across the floor, and, as it did so, Felicia reached out a hand and scratched Charlotte on the arm with her sharp nails.

"Ouch!" cried Charlotte. She was taken aback, and for the first time she was angry with Felicia. "I thought you were my friend," she said. "And I thought you were playing a game, not catching mice."

"You spoiled my game," replied Felicia.

Bozo had been freed from the cellar, and he was barking. Tony was calling, "Charlotte! Felicia! The party is over!" Felicia slipped her hand into Charlotte's, but Charlotte drew hers away. As they walked, a little apart, toward the lighted kitchen, she wondered if she and Felicia could be friends any more.

The End of Felicia's Visit

John's visit was over, but not Felicia's. John's father and mother came to fetch him on Saturday, but Felicia's mother, who was the cat in Mr. Green's store, stayed right where she was.

"I can't imagine a mother abandoning her child," Mrs. Fairlee said to Dr. Fairlee. The doctor had put an advertisement in the *Linton Gazette*, appealing to Felicia's parents, or other relatives, to come to his house and claim her. There hadn't been any reply so far, but Dr. and Mrs. Fairlee were still hoping for one.

In the meantime, Charlotte was at her wits' end. She didn't want Felicia to scratch her again, but she didn't want to report her naughtiness to her mother and father. It isn't Felicia's fault that she is a cat, she thought; and she said to herself, "I still like cats, but it's hard to have a cat for company all the time when we are really so different."

Felicia, in turn, was restless and fidgety. She declared that the preparations for school made her nervous.

"We have to go to school," said Charlotte. Her father had spoken to her very forcefully about going to school, and, as a matter of fact, she was beginning to look forward to seeing her school friends again.

Mrs. Fairlee had bought each of the children a satchel and a pencil box, and she said that she was going to talk to the school principal. Charlotte guessed that Felicia would be the subject of their talk, and she wondered if she ought to tell her mother, right now, that Felicia was a cat.

Charlotte no longer felt honor bound to keep Felicia's secret, since Felicia, more than once, had done forbidden things. At the same time, Charlotte felt sorry for Felicia, who didn't *look* like a cat and didn't *act* like a little girl.

She decided to speak to Felicia instead of to her mother. "Don't you wish, sometimes, that you still looked like a cat?" she asked her.

"Oh, I can look like a cat any time I please," said Felicia. *"That* part isn't hard. But I can't make up my mind exactly what to do. I don't want to stay in this house and go to school, and I don't want to go back to the woods and live by myself." Then a purring note came into her voice, as she asked, coaxingly, "Would you mind asking your mother to take us to Westover again? I mean, before school begins?"

Charlotte didn't mind at all. She knew that

her mother was going to see the school principal that afternoon and that she was planning to take Tony with her to Westover, because he needed some new shoes. "I'll ask Mother right away," she said to Felicia.

Mrs. Fairlee said that of course the girls might go to Westover, too. She had planned to buy Tony's shoes first, and then go to the school. "You children can all stay together while I talk to the principal," she said. Then, as Charlotte went to tell Felicia, Mrs. Fairlee wrote a note and pinned it on the front door. The note was for Felicia's father and mother in case they should come to the house while everyone was away.

Felicia put on her calico dress, the dress she had first appeared in. She washed her face by rubbing it with a rough, dry cloth. "I'm ready to go to Westover," she said to Charlotte.

"You had better put on your shoes," said Charlotte.

So Felicia put on her sneakers.

The hay had been carted away from the fields, but Tony sneezed all the way to West-over. "You ought to have worn your sweater, Tony," said Mrs. Fairlee.

Charlotte made no comment, and neither did Felicia. But Felicia was smiling, and there was a light in her green eyes. "I wonder if she has made up her mind," Charlotte said to herself.

Mrs. Fairlee parked her station wagon behind the row of shops, and told the children to hop out. "You girls can wait outside, if you like," she said, as she and Tony went into the shoe store.

"Let's look in windows," Charlotte said to Felicia. She had already spied the calico cat in the grocery store window. It was sunning itself between two pyramids of fruit, and it looked well-fed and sleek. Charlotte was sure that Mr. Green gave it plenty of things to eat. It probably catches mice during the night, too, she thought.

The cat blinked its green eyes lazily. "It's looking at us, Felicia," said Charlotte.

But Felicia was not beside her. Charlotte glanced up and down the street, but she didn't see her anywhere. Then she went inside the grocery store, thinking that Felicia must have whisked in there.

The store was filled with customers, and Mr. Green and his assistants were all busy. Felicia was nowhere in sight, and Charlotte went to look among the crates and packing boxes at the rear of the store.

"Are you looking for something, Charlotte?" asked Mr. Green.

"Yes. Have you seen a little girl with black hair?" asked Charlotte.

"Let me see," said Mr. Green. "I've been so busy. . . . But I *do* remember a little girl coming into the store. She isn't here now, though."

"No," said Charlotte. "She doesn't seem to be here."

Just as Mr. Green went off to wait on a customer, Charlotte suddenly noticed a pair of small white sneakers. They were placed neatly on a carton that was partly hidden by a big wooden packing box.

Felicia's sneakers, thought Charlotte.

"Don't tell," whispered a voice. Then Charlotte saw Felicia herself, behind the same packing box. But Felicia didn't look the way she usually did. She seemed to be smaller, and her eyes looked more catlike.

"What's happening to you, Felicia?" asked Charlotte anxiously.

Felicia began to purr. She was becoming even smaller. And, before Charlotte's astonished eyes, her printed calico dress turned into fur, and her black hair turned into fur, too. Her ribbon bows, which Charlotte had so often admired, became two ears—and there was Felicia, a little cat again! Charlotte reached out to pat her, but she would not stay to be patted. Off she slipped through a narrow passage between two crates, without even one backward look.

Charlotte felt dazed for a moment. She touched Felicia's sneakers, which had been bought for a little girl, not a little cat. They were all that Felicia had left behind. They didn't belong to Charlotte, and she decided to leave them where they were.

Charlotte went out to the sidewalk again. There were two cats in the window now, two calico cats, and Charlotte saw that one was a good deal smaller than the other. It was a middle-sized cat, exactly like the one she had met on the hillside under the elm tree. The black markings on its head looked like black hair parted in the middle, and its perky ears resembled a little girl's hair bows.

There she is, thought Charlotte. She was glad to see that both cats had smiling expressions on their faces, as if they were very pleased at being together again.

"Where is Felicia?" asked Mrs. Fairlee, when she and Tony had emerged from the shoe store.

"She found her mother," said Charlotte, happily.

"Really and truly?" asked Mrs. Fairlee.

"Really and truly," said Charlotte.

"Her mother must have read the advertisement in the paper, and come to the house and found my note," said Mrs. Fairlee. Then she asked, "What did Felicia's mother look like, Charlotte?"

"She looked almost the same as Felicia," replied Charlotte.

The birds came back, Bozo stopped barking, and Tony stopped sneezing, because there was no longer a cat child visiting the Fairlees. But the family often spoke of the green-eyed little girl who had appeared among them so suddenly.

One day Mrs. Fairlee said to Charlotte, "For some reason, Felicia always reminded me of a cat."

She *almost* guessed, thought Charlotte. But she had kept Felicia's secret all this time, so all she said was, "Yes, Felicia *was* rather like a cat."